D1279666

Monster Boy's Soccer Game

BY CARL EMERSON
ILLUSTRATED BY LON LEVIN

magic wagon

visit us at www.abdopublishing.com

Published by Magic Wagon, a division of the ABDO Publishing Group, 8000 West 78th Street, Edina, Minnesota 55439. Copyright © 2009 by Abdo Consulting Group, Inc. International copyrights reserved in all countries. All rights reserved. No part of this book may be reproduced in any form without written permission from the publisher.

Looking Glass Library™ is a trademark and logo of Magic Wagon.

Printed in the United States.

Text by Carl Emerson
Illustrations by Lon Levin
Edited by Patricia Stockland
Interior layout and design by Emily Love
Cover design by Emily Love

Library of Congress Cataloging-in-Publication Data
Emerson, Carl.
 Monster Boy's soccer game / by Carl Emerson ; illustrated by Lon Levin.
    p. cm. — (Monster Boy)
 ISBN 978-1-60270-239-4 (alk. paper)
 [1. Monsters—Fiction. 2. Soccer—Fiction.] I. Levin, Lon, ill. II. Title.
 PZ7.E582Mq 2008
 [E]—dc22

                    2008003778

Mr. and Mrs. Onster watched as their son, Marty, played. Marty picked up a stuffed animal and spoke softly to it.

"Oh Sassafrass, you're my favorite!" he said.

"Monte, what is he doing?" Mrs. Onster asked her husband.

"I think he's . . . he's cuddling his stuffed puppy," Mr. Onster replied.

Mrs. Onster suddenly felt very ill.

"Why isn't he tearing it limb from limb?" she cried. "Why isn't he trying to eat it? Why isn't he at least slobbering all over it?"

Mr. and Mrs. Onster had been trying to raise their son to be just like them.

They took him to monster class three nights a week. There, he learned to snarl and slobber. He was taught how to make noises under little children's beds. He was also given toenail chips and scum pudding for snacks.

But he was still just a boy— not a budding monster.

"Oh, Monte, what can we do?" Mrs. Onster sighed. "We have to find something to help him become the monster we know he can be."

Just then, Mr. Onster saw something in the local newspaper. "Martha, I may have just the thing."

Mr. Onster showed his wife the newspaper.

"Maybe if we get him involved in sports the true monster in him will come out," Mr. Onster said.

Later that day, Mr. and Mrs. Onster signed Marty up for soccer.

Before Marty's first practice, Mr. and Mrs. Onster gave him some advice.

"Now Marty," Mr. Onster said, "if you have the ball and other players get in your way, run right over them."

"And Marty," Mrs. Onster said, "if someone on the other team scores a goal, go ahead and eat him."

"I don't want to eat anyone," Marty said. "I just want to have fun playing soccer, like the other kids."

That was NOT what Mr. and Mrs. Onster wanted to hear. But they promised to watch him play anyway.

The next day, Marty went to his first practice. He was very happy to see that his best friend, Sally Weet, was on his team. He was also happy to see that Bart Ully was on a different team.

During practices, Marty learned all the rules of soccer.
He also learned how to be a good teammate.

"When you get the ball, look for a teammate to pass it
to," the coach said. Marty always passed the ball. He
learned to play good defense. He never ran over anyone,
even when his team practiced against Bart's team.

Finally, it was time for his team's first game. Marty was excited to show what a good teammate he was.

The first time he got the ball, Marty passed it to Sally. She scored!

The second time he got the ball, someone from the other team stole it.

Marty started to get a funny feeling inside.

The next time Marty tried to pass, the ball was stolen again! The other team scored a goal.

Suddenly, Marty did not feel well. It was like his insides were turning upside down. His eyes felt hot and his skin felt thick. Marty realized he was panting. But he couldn't make it stop.

The next time Marty got the ball, he was a panting, slobbery, snotty mess.

Marty was not going to pass or try dribbling the ball around anyone, either. He snarled as he took the ball over and through the defense. He wound up and fired a shot. The ball screamed into the goal.

Marty's coach saw what was happening. He decided that Marty might be better playing in goal.

"Maybe playing in the field isn't the right spot for you," the coach said. "I bet you could do a good job of stopping the other team from scoring."

Marty's team was doing well. With time almost out, Marty's team led 2-1.

Suddenly, a boy from the other team broke through the defense. He ran in for a shot to tie the game. Marty's hair stood on end. His forehead crinkled. His claws poked out.

The ball sailed toward a corner of the goal. Marty dove and made an amazing save.

The referee's whistle blew. Time was up. His teammates jumped for joy.

Marty wasn't slimy, slobbery, or snarly anymore. He was just a little sheepish.

"Sorry about the ball, Coach," he said.

"That's okay, Marty," said the coach, smiling. "I guess you're a real soccer animal!"

Contain Your Inner Monster
Tips from Marty Onster

- Play sports that get your heart pumping.

- Take a break from a situation that is making you upset.

- Count to ten and take deep breaths to calm down when something or someone is upsetting you.

- When you keep your temper, reward yourself with snacks of snail shells and pond scum!